MY Panda SWEATER

WRITTEN BY **Gilles Baum**   ILLUSTRATED BY **Barroux**

TRANSLATED BY **Lisa Rosinsky**

Barefoot Books
step inside a story

I love my lucky panda sweater!
I wear it all the time, even in the summer.

At school, at dance class —
I'm a panda bear everywhere.
I don't care if the other kids laugh.

All I need to do is pull up my panda hood . . .
and right away, everything feels better.

But my lucky panda sweater starts to shrink.
Or maybe I'm growing. One day, it doesn't fit anymore.

Mama suggests I put it in the box of clothes to give away.
"Now that you're older," she says, "it's time to share your
lucky clothes with others."

That makes me think. I start to notice what people wear.
I wonder about the stories behind their clothes.

I notice that Mr. Arnaz's shoes are much too big.

Maybe they're lucky, too! Maybe a clown gave them to him . . .
giant shoes so he can take giant steps towards happiness.

At the market, Somya the spoon-seller
always wears the same scarf.

Maybe Dr. Mullins gave it to her on a rainy day! He makes her smile, so she doesn't mind if the scarf doesn't match her outfit.

At school, Ziggy always wears the same sports shirt.

Maybe his superstar Uncle Ken gave him that shirt, to remind him that he's a star, too.

Then one day, I see my lucky panda sweater again!
Under the hood, I see a girl with tired eyes.

She sits next to me. She doesn't say a word.

Our desk shakes a little as she scribbles hard in
her notebook. I wonder what her story is.

I want to tell her the story of my panda sweater.
That it brings good luck. That I'm glad she has it now,
and I hope she'll always feel safe inside it, too.

When the bell rings, everyone runs out to the
playground. Except us. I smile at my panda friend.
She smiles back.

In our empty classroom, I turn on some music.
We dance together.

A few people are watching,
maybe even laughing at us,
but we don't care.

We are panda bears
and we are not alone.

Many things we own get thrown away when they can be used again. If you can't reuse something yourself, try to find someone who might appreciate having it. This can mean sharing books with friends, giving toys you no longer play with to younger siblings, or donating clothes you've outgrown to a charity.

Passing on clothes and other objects to someone else when you no longer need them gives others a chance to have something that they might need, and also keeps waste out of landfill sites. If you want to donate some of the things you're finished with, ask a parent, guardian or teacher to help you.

For Anne and her washing machine — G. B.

Barefoot Books
2067 Massachusetts Ave
Cambridge, MA 02140

Barefoot Books
29/30 Fitzroy Square
London, W1T 6LQ

Reproduction by Bright Arts, Hong Kong
Printed in China on 100% acid-free paper
This book was typeset in Blockhead, Chalkduster and Mr Lucky
The illustrations were prepared in acrylics on paper with some collages

Original French text copyright © 2017 by Gilles Baum
Illustrations copyright © 2017 by Barroux
First published in France as *Mon pull panda* © Éditions Kilowatt, 2017
Translation copyright © 2020 by Lisa Rosinsky
The moral rights of Gilles Baum and Barroux have been asserted

Hardback ISBN 978-1-78285-979-6
Paperback ISBN 978-1-78285-980-2
E-book ISBN 978-1-64686-022-7

Graphic design by Sarah Soldano, Barefoot Books
English-language edition edited by Kate DePalma, Barefoot Books
Translated by Lisa Rosinsky

British Cataloguing-in-Publication Data:
a catalogue record for this book is available from the British Library

Library of Congress Cataloging-in-Publication Data
is available under 2019044629

1 3 5 7 9 8 6 4 2

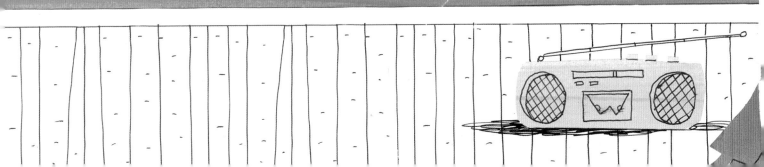

Barefoot Books
Step inside a story

At Barefoot Books, we celebrate art and story that opens the hearts and minds of children from all walks of life, focusing on themes that encourage independence of spirit, enthusiasm for learning and respect for the world's diversity. The welfare of our children is dependent on the welfare of the planet, so we source paper from sustainably managed forests and constantly strive to reduce our environmental impact. Playful, beautiful and created to last a lifetime, our products combine the best of the present with the best of the past to educate our children as the caretakers of tomorrow.

www.barefootbooks.com

Gilles Baum studied mathematics and became a school teacher after his plans of becoming a superhero and conquering the world fell through. Inspired by his students, he writes for children so they may live all the exciting lives that he wasn't able to. Gilles lives in Alsace, France.

Born in Paris and raised in Morocco, **Barroux** returned to France to study art and work as an art director. He began his career as an illustrator after moving to Montreal. Barroux has illustrated many children's books, including *I Could Be, You Could Be* for Barefoot Books.